SEE HOW PLANTS GROW
Leaves

Nicola Edwards

PowerKiDS press.

New York

Published in 2008 by The Rosen Publishing Group, Inc.
29 East 21st Street, New York, NY 10010

First Edition

The publishers would like to thank the following for allowing us to reproduce their pictures in this book:
Alamy: cover (David J King), 22 (Dave King/dk). Corbis: title page and 14 (Phil Schermeister), 5 (Nigel J. Dennis/Gallo Images), 6 (Gavriel Jecan), 7 (Andrianna Williams/zefa), 8 (Dietrich Rose/zefa), 11 (John M Roberts), 12 (Michael Boys), 13 (Micro Discovery), 15 (Gary Braasch), 16 (Tony Craddock/zefa), 18, 20 (Hugh Sitton/zefa), 21 (Dallas & John Heaton/Free Agents Ltd). Ecoscene: 4 (Joel Creed), 19 (Sally Morgan). Getty Images: 17 (Taxi). NHPA: 23 (Stephen Krasemann). Nature Picture Library: 9 (Larry Michael). Science Photo Library: 10 (Steve Taylor).

Library of Congress Cataloging-in-Publication Data
Edwards, Nicola.
  Leaves / Nicola Edwards. -- 1st ed.
      p. cm. -- (See how plants grow)
  Includes index.
  ISBN-13: 978-1-0-4042-3703-2 (library binding)
  ISBN-10: 1-4042-3703-8 (library binding)
  1. Leaves--Juvenile literature. I. Title.
  QK649.E39 2007
  581.4'8--dc22
                                                    2006026544

Manufactured in China

Contents

What Are leaves?

Leaves grow on plants, mostly above the ground, although they can grow underwater, too. Leaves are important parts of plants. Plants breathe through their leaves and leaves make food for the growing plants.

▼ The huge leaves of the Amazon water lily measure around seven feet (two meters) across.

Green-leaved plants provide food for people and animals. We eat the leaves themselves or other parts of the plants, such as their **fruit** or **seeds**.

▲ With its thick lips and long tongue, this giraffe can eat the leaves of tall, prickly trees.

What do leaves look like?

Leaves can be huge or tiny, long or short, wide or narrow. They can have smooth or jagged edges, sharp points, or rounded ends. Some leaves are sticky or have a waxy surface.

▲ How many different leaf shapes can you see in this area of rain forest?

Leaf Fact

Not all leaves are green. The leaves of the Poinsettia plant, for example, are red.

Tubes called **veins** run through a leaf. Like the bones in our bodies, these veins support the leaf.

▲ The veins take water and **nutrients** to every part of the leaf.

7

Leaves in hot and cold areas

Leaves vary in different parts of the world. Thin, needlelike leaves grow on **conifers** in cold areas.

▼ Can you see the needlelike leaves on this conifer?

Plants need water to grow. In dry areas, leaves are sometimes covered in hairs, spines, or scales. This helps to stop the plants from losing too much water.

▲ These prickly spines are the leaves of the cactus plant.

How do leaves start to grow?

When a seed is planted underground, it needs water, warmth, and usually soil to grow. The seed **germinates** and begins to grow. A shoot carrying the plant's first leaves pushes upward from it. These leaves were part of the seed, which contained food to fuel growth.

You can see this sunflower plant's first leaves appearing through the soil.

Leaf Fact

Leaves use water, sunlight, and **carbon dioxide** to make food for plants.

▲ As new leaves grow, they take over the job of making food for the developing plant.

What are leaves for?

Leaves make food for the growing plant. They allow the plant to breathe, and they control the amount of water it contains.

▲ Rhubarb leaves store water for the growing plant.

Leaf Fact

Plants can take in nutrients and gases through their leaves, even if they are growing underwater.

Leaves have tiny holes called **stomata** on their undersides. These holes can open and close to allow gases—carbon dioxide, **oxygen**, and **water vapor**—to pass in and out of the leaf.

▲ In this picture, the stomata have been magnified many times so that you can see them clearly.

How do leaves make food?

Leaves contain **chlorophyll**. This gives them their green color and helps them to make food. The leaves use energy from sunlight. This energy turns water from the soil and carbon dioxide from the air into food for the plant.

▼ The chlorophyll in leaves helps them to make food.

When leaves make food, they produce a gas called oxygen. We need to breathe oxygen to live.

These fern leaves, called fronds, grow in a pattern to make sure that each leaf receives as much sunlight as possible.

How do leaves change?

The leaves of **broad-leaved trees** change in the fall as the days become colder. Their color changes from green to gold, red, and brown. The leaves fall from the branches and the trees remain bare during the winter. In springtime, as the days become warmer, leaf buds grow on the branches.

▲ Leaf buds start to open to reveal new leaves.

Leaf Fact

In the fall, the chlorophyll fades from the leaves, allowing other colors to show through.

How many colors can you see in these leaves?

Defense and attack

Some leaves have ways to stop animals from eating them. They may have prickly edges, like holly, or stinging hairs, like nettles.

The sharp, spiky edges of these holly leaves stop hungry animals from coming too close!

Some leaves, such as thyme, contain strong-smelling oils that make animals avoid them. The leaves of meat-eating plants can trap their prey.

The hinged leaves of this Venus flytrap snap shut, trapping insects inside them.

How do we use leaves?

We can eat leaves, such as spinach and cabbage, raw or cooked. We use the fresh and dried leaves of scented herbs like mint to add flavor to food. Leaves are used to make medicines, too. The dried leaves of the coconut palm are woven or braided and made into baskets and mats.

The dye used to make these decorative patterns comes from the crushed leaves of the henna plant.

These leaves are used to make tea, one of the world's favorite drinks.

Grow your own leaves

You can grow all kinds of leafy plants from seeds. You could grow cress, basil, or dill and then taste the leaves.

Fill a pot with soil and sprinkle a few seeds on top. Then cover the seeds with soil.

▲ You could also try soaking bean seeds in water and then plant them. The tiny leaves inside each seed will begin to grow.

Leaf Fact

Some leaves are poisonous. Don't touch any leaves until you are sure they are safe.

Water the soil gently and keep it damp.
Put the pot in a
warm place and
watch your
plant grow.

▼ Can you see
the roots of this
bean seedling?

Glossary

broad-leaved trees
Trees that have wide, flat leaves and produce flowers and fruit.

carbon dioxide
A gas in air that leaves use to make food.

chlorophyll
The substance that gives leaves their green color and helps them to make food.

conifers
Trees with thin, spiny leaves.

fruit
The part of a plant that contains seeds.

germinate
When a seed starts to develop into a plant.

nutrients
Food in the soil that a plant needs for growth.

oxygen
A gas that leaves produce when they make food. People need to breathe oxygen to live.

seeds
The parts of a plant from which new plants develop.

stomata
Holes in the underside of a leaf through which gases pass in and out.

veins
Tubes in a leaf that carry water and nutrients to every part of it.

water vapor
Water in the form of a gas.

Web Sites

Due to the changing nature of Internet links, PowerKids Press has developed an online list of Web sites related to the subject of this book. This site is regularly updated. Please use this link to access this list: www.powerkidslinks.com/shpg/leaves/

Index